How It's Done

Making an Animated Movie

by Wendy Hinote Lanier

FOCUS READERS

BEACON

www.focusreaders.com

Focus Readers is distributed by North Star Editions:
sales@northstareditions.com | 888-417-0195

Produced for Focus Readers by Red Line Editorial.

Content Consultant: Brian J. Larson, Associate Professor and Animation Program Director, School of Film and Animation, Rochester Institute of Technology

Photographs ©: mediaphotos/iStockphoto, cover, 1; Dean Drobot/Shutterstock Images, 4; Sarunyu L/Shutterstock Images, 7, 29; Alastair Grant/AP Images, 8; smolaw11/iStockphoto, 10; Chaosamran_Studio/Shutterstock Images, 13; Ma. Amanda A.S.Gana/Shutterstock Images, 14; Ihor Biliavskyi/Shutterstock Images, 17 (left); Heather Woollard/Shutterstock Images, 17 (right); Mahmud Hams/AFP/Getty Images, 18; Iryna Imago/Shutterstock Images, 20–21; BartekSzewczyk/iStockphoto, 22; Firstsignal/iStockphoto, 25; Walt Disney Animation Studios/Album/Alamy, 26

Library of Congress Cataloging-in-Publication Data
Names: Hinote Lanier, Wendy, 1963- author.
Title: Making an animated movie / by Wendy Hinote Lanier.
Description: Lake Elmo, MN : Focus Readers, [2020] | Series: How it's done | Includes index. | Audience: Grades 4–6.
Identifiers: LCCN 2019033118 (print) | LCCN 2019033119 (ebook) | ISBN 9781644930397 (hardcover) | ISBN 9781644931189 (paperback) | ISBN 9781644932766 (pdf) | ISBN 9781644931974 (ebook)
Subjects: LCSH: Animation (Cinematography)--Juvenile literature.
Classification: LCC TR897.5 .H56 2020 (print) | LCC TR897.5 (ebook) | DDC 777/.7--dc23
LC record available at https://lccn.loc.gov/2019033118
LC ebook record available at https://lccn.loc.gov/2019033119

Printed in the United States of America
Mankato, MN
012020

About the Author

Wendy Hinote Lanier is a former elementary teacher and a Texan through and through. She writes and speaks for children and adults on a variety of topics. She is the author of more than 40 books for children and young adults on topics related to science, technology, social studies, the arts, and, of course, Texas.

Table of Contents

Chapter 1

At the Movies

Excitement is in the air. A new animated movie is playing at the local theater. People buy popcorn and drinks. Then they take their seats. The lights go out. Soon, the movie begins.

Going to the movies is a fun event for many people.

Characters appear on the screen. They seem completely lifelike. Everyone is caught up in the story. They forget the characters are not real.

An animated movie uses the voices of real people. But the characters are artwork. Teams

Fun Fact

The first full-length animated movie was released in 1917. A house fire destroyed the only copy.

Animated characters are drawn by artists and brought to life on computers.

of artists create each character. They use computers to bring the characters to life. This process takes time. A full-length movie can take months or even years to make.

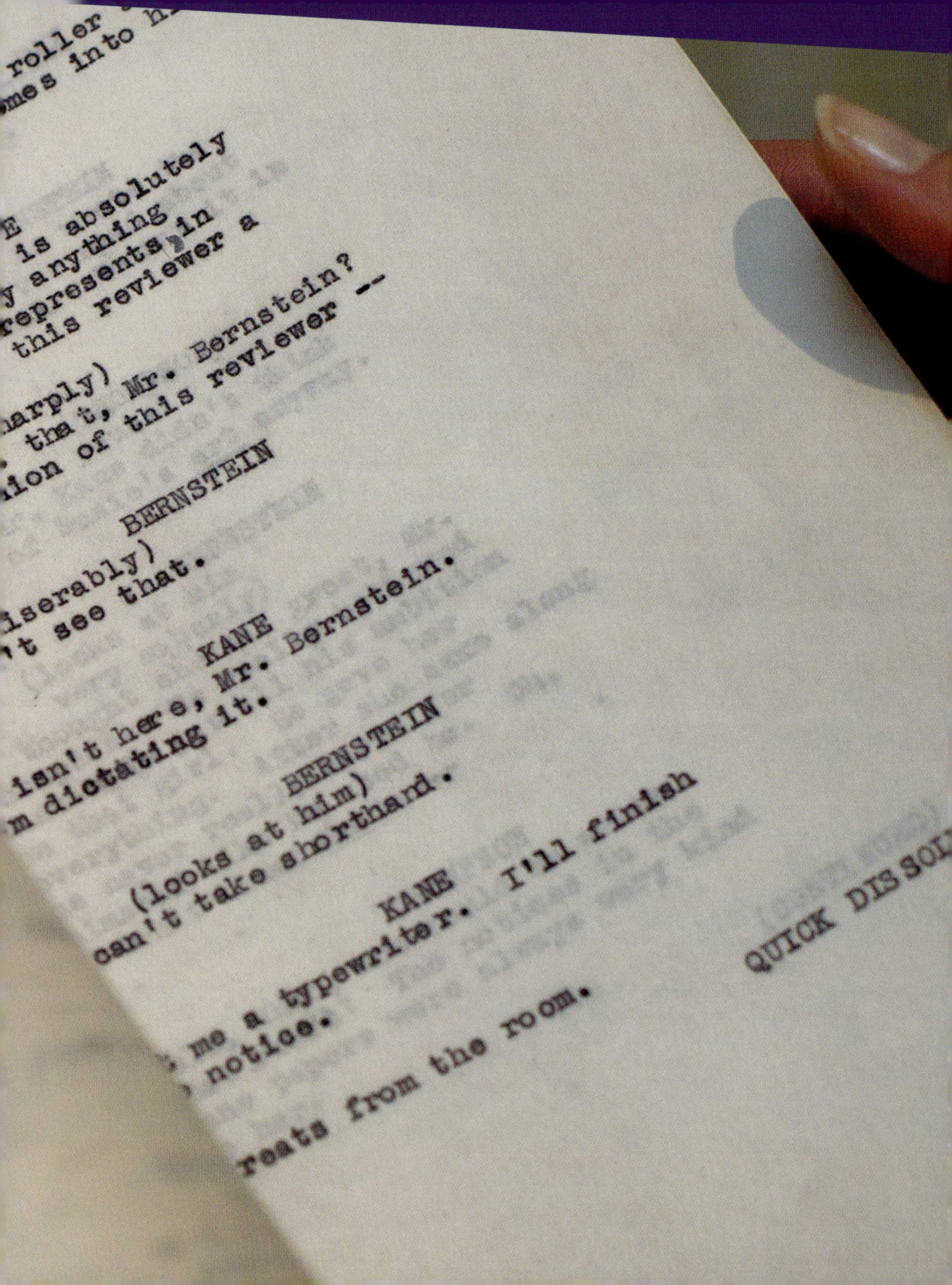

roller
is absolutely
anything
represents in
this reviewer a
Mr. Bernstein?
that, Mr. Bernstein
of this reviewer --
BERNSTEIN
see that.
KANE
here, Mr. Bernstein.
dictating it.
BERNSTEIN
(looks at him)
can't take shorthand.
KANE
me a typewriter. I'll finish
notice.
from the room.
QUICK

Chapter 2

Getting Started

An animated movie starts with a script. A script is a movie in written form. It explains what all of the characters say and do. Artists use the script to create a storyboard.

Most movie scripts are more than 100 pages long.

A storyboard includes drawings and notes about each scene.

A storyboard is a series of drawings. It shows the major **scenes** and camera shots. Notes describe what should happen in each scene. The notes could be about characters' actions or location changes. The **director** decides how the movie will flow.

Next, a story team works on the scenes. Team members decide the best order for the scenes. Then they create an animatic. The animatic is made up of the storyboard's still pictures. It also includes temporary voices, music, and sound effects. The animatic shows where the dialogue should go. It gives the director a feel for how long each scene should be.

The director may make changes. But eventually the director approves the script and the animatic. Then voice actors record the dialogue. This step happens even before the characters are designed.

Next, a team of artists gets to work. They finalize the designs for

Fun Fact

Toy Story was the first fully 3D-animated movie made using computers. It was released in 1995.

Artists create detailed designs for each character.

characters and backgrounds. They make detailed drawings called model sheets. These sheets show how each character will look and move. Soon the movie is ready for **production**.

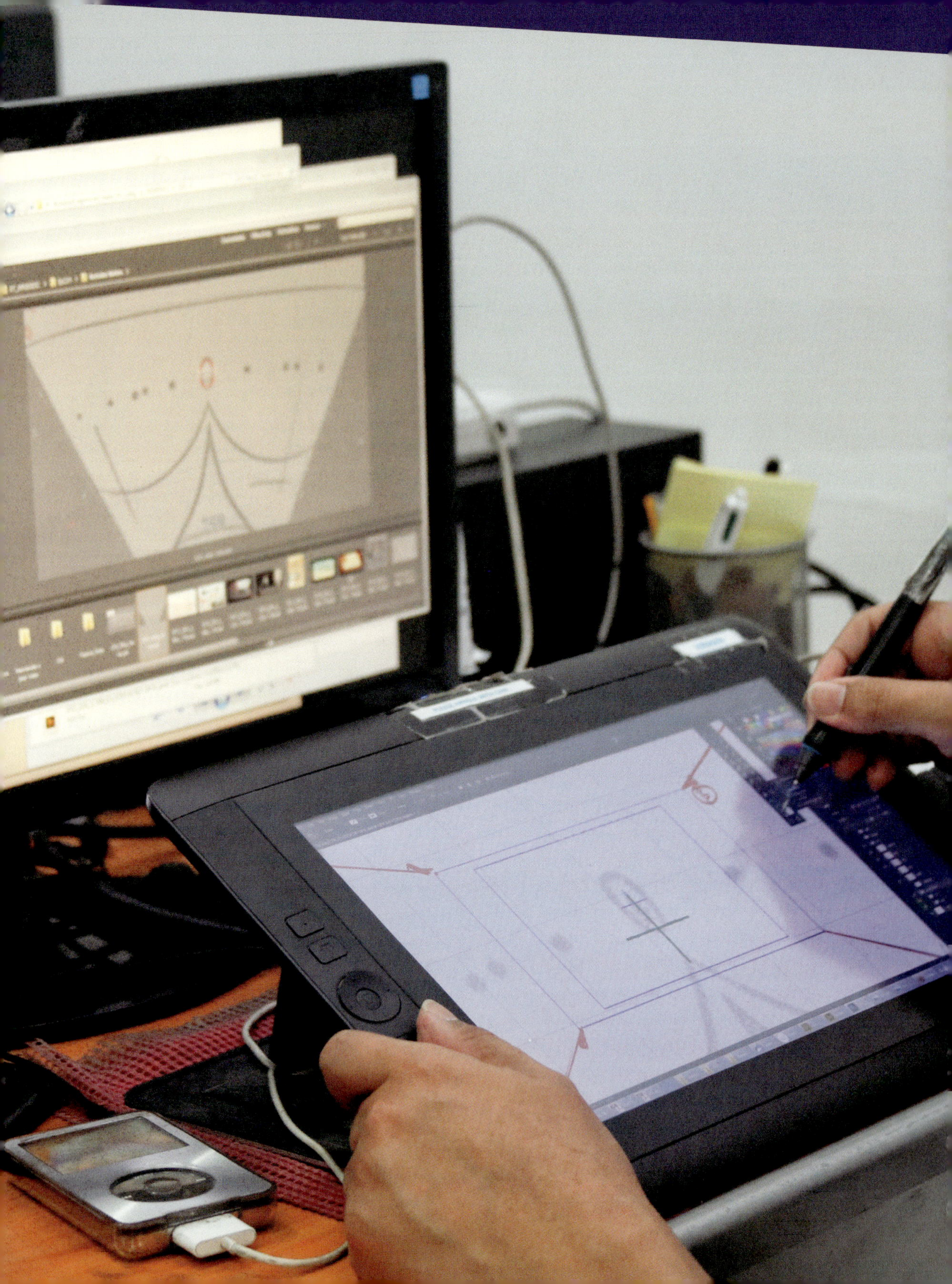

Chapter 3

Production of 3D Animation

As production begins, artists create a layout. The layout is like a 3D animatic. Artists plan each shot. They decide where characters and objects will go. They choose camera angles.

Artists create the layout on computers.

Artists use rough 3D models or blocks. These models stand in place of characters and **settings**.

Next, the layout goes to the modeling team. Some modelers work on characters. Others work on backgrounds and objects. The modelers study the model sheets. Then they turn those designs into 3D models. The new computer models are just shapes. They have no color. The director must approve these completed models.

2D VS. 3D ANIMATION

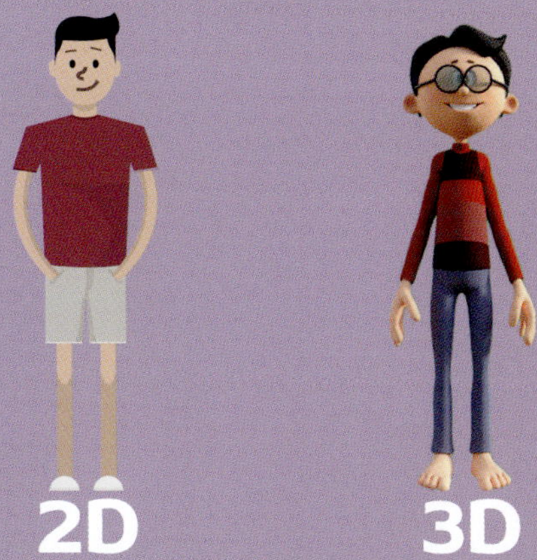

3D animation is just one form of animation. Some movies are made with 2D animation. A 2D picture is flat, like a drawing. *Snow White* and *The Little Mermaid* are examples of 2D animation. However, 3D animation has become more common. A 3D character appears to take up space. It has depth. *The Incredibles* and *Zootopia* are examples of 3D animation.

Then, the 3D models go to the surface team. Artists add color and shading details. They add texture to show how surfaces might feel.

With modeling and shading, the characters on screen become more complex and lifelike.

The **rigging** team then gives each character model a 3D skeleton. The riggers also create controls for moving the skeletons. The characters become like puppets.

The riggers send the characters to the animation team. **Animators** use the controls that the riggers made. They make the characters move and talk. They tell the story of the movie through the actions of the characters. They follow the images from the storyboard.

Fun Fact

Walt Disney was a famous animator in the 1900s. His first successful character was a rabbit named Oswald.

THAT'S AMAZING!

Stop-Motion Animation

One type of animation is stop-motion, which uses photographs of real objects. The objects are usually 10 inches (25 cm) tall or shorter. People move the objects slightly between each photo. They take many photos. A movie shows the photos in order. The objects in the photos appear to move.

People have been creating stop-motion movies since 1898. In 1925, a movie called *The Lost World* used stop-motion dinosaurs. They were so lifelike that some people believed they were real.

People can make their own stop-motion movies.

Chapter 4

Final Changes

At every step, the director and animation supervisors review the project. They make sure the scenes flow smoothly. Sometimes they decide to remove scenes that aren't as important to the story.

The director may ask for changes throughout a project.

Their work keeps the project moving forward. And after many months, the movie is almost complete.

Each day, lighting artists work to update the film. They add lights and colors to the shots. They look at camera movements and shading.

Fun Fact

Some animation takes research. For example, *Shrek* animators took mud showers. They studied how mud dripped.

Lighting artists make sure the lighting in each scene looks realistic.

They make sure the lighting in each scene creates the right mood.

Compositing creates the final look of the film. In this process, compositors combine the work from other teams in each scene.

People work to make sure sounds match the characters' lip movements.

They fix color problems. They make sure the actions look believable.

Music and sound effects are added last. The sound effects and **lip sync** must be correct. Any changes made after final edits could throw the timing off.

A full-length animated movie can take more than a year to make. Hundreds of people are involved. Some work only with computers. Others create models and drawings by hand. But together they make movie magic.

Fun Fact

One second of animation takes 24 images. And it takes six to eight weeks to produce 60 seconds. Busy scenes can take even longer. Many people work together to make a movie.

FOCUS ON

Making an Animated Movie

Write your answers on a separate piece of paper.

1. Write a sentence that describes the main idea of Chapter 3.
2. What part of making an animated movie do you think you would be best at? Why?
3. What is the first step for an animated movie?
   - **A.** a model
   - **B.** a song
   - **C.** a script
4. What would happen if the rigging department failed to correctly rig a character?
   - **A.** The animators would not be able to make the character move.
   - **B.** The animators would make the character the wrong color.
   - **C.** The animators would have to get rid of a character.

5. What does **texture** mean in this book?

*They add **texture** to show how surfaces might feel.*

- **A.** how hot or cold something is
- **B.** the feel or appearance of a surface
- **C.** the background setting of an object

6. What does **puppets** mean in this book?

*The riggers also create controls for moving the skeletons. The characters become like **puppets**.*

- **A.** beings under someone else's control
- **B.** people who can control others
- **C.** dolls that move and act on their own

Answer key on page 32.

Glossary

animators
Artists who create several images of a single character. The character appears to move when those images are viewed quickly one after another.

compositing
The combining of images from different teams (such as characters, background, objects, etc.) into one image.

director
A person who is in charge of making a movie.

lip sync
The matching of lip movements with sounds or voices.

production
The part of the animated movie–making process that involves modeling, rigging, and animation.

rigging
A computer-generated skeleton used to create movement in an animated character.

scenes
The separate places and times shown throughout a movie or play.

settings
The places where scenes happen.

To Learn More

BOOKS

Bellmont, Laura. *Animation Lab for Kids: Fun Projects for Visual Storytelling and Making Art Move.* Beverly, MA: Quarto Publishing, 2016.

Slater, Lee. *John Lasseter: Director of* Toy Story. Minneapolis: Abdo Publishing, 2017.

Suen, Anastasia. *Video Animation and Photography.* Vero Beach, FL: Rourke Educational Media, 2017.

NOTE TO EDUCATORS

Visit **www.focusreaders.com** to find lesson plans, activities, links, and other resources related to this title.

Index

Answer Key: 1. Answers will vary; **2.** Answers will vary; **3.** C; **4.** A; **5.** B; **6.** A